PUFFIN BOOKS

Sheltie by the

Make friends with

Sheltie

The little pony with the big heart

Sheltie is the lovable little Shetland pony with a big personality. His best friend and owner is Emma, and together they have lots of exciting adventures.

Share Sheltie and Emma's adventures in

SHELTIE THE SHETLAND PONY
SHELTIE SAVES THE DAY
SHELTIE AND THE RUNAWAY
SHELTIE FINDS A FRIEND
SHELTIE TO THE RESCUE
SHELTIE IN DANGER
SHELTIE RIDES TO WIN
SHELTIE AND THE SADDLE MYSTERY
SHELTIE LEADS THE WAY
SHELTIE THE HERO
SHELTIE IN TROUBLE
SHELTIE AND THE STRAY
SHELTIE AND THE SNOW PONY
SHELTIE ON PARADE
SHELTIE FOR EVER
SHELTIE ON PATROL

Peter Clover was born and went to school in London. He was a storyboard artist and illustrator before he began to put words to his pictures. He enjoys painting, travelling, cooking and keeping fit, and lives on the coast in Somerset.

Also by Peter Clover in Puffin

The Sheltie series

1: SHELTIE THE SHETLAND PONY
2: SHELTIE SAVES THE DAY
3: SHELTIE AND THE RUNAWAY
4: SHELTIE FINDS A FRIEND
5: SHELTIE TO THE RESCUE
6: SHELTIE IN DANGER
7: SHELTIE RIDES TO WIN
8: SHELTIE AND THE SADDLE MYSTERY
9: SHELTIE LEADS THE WAY
10: SHELTIE THE HERO
11: SHELTIE IN TROUBLE
12: SHELTIE AND THE STRAY
13: SHELTIE AND THE SNOW PONY
14: SHELTIE ON PARADE
15: SHELTIE FOR EVER
16: SHELTIE ON PATROL
17: SHELTIE GOES TO SCHOOL
18: SHELTIE GALLOPS AHEAD
19: SHELTIE IN DOUBLE TROUBLE
20: SHELTIE IN PERIL

Sheltie
by the Sea

Peter Clover

PUFFIN BOOKS

*To all my special readers
at the Hillside Learning Centre*

PUFFIN BOOKS

Published by the Penguin Group
Penguin Books Ltd, 27 Wrights Lane, London W8 5TZ, England
Penguin Putnam Inc., 375 Hudson Street, New York, New York 10014, USA
Penguin Books Australia Ltd, Ringwood, Victoria, Australia
Penguin Books Canada Ltd, 10 Alcorn Avenue, Toronto, Ontario, Canada M4V 3B2
Penguin Books (NZ) Ltd, Private Bag 102902, NSMC, Auckland, New Zealand

On the World Wide Web at: www.penguin.com

Penguin Books Ltd, Registered Offices: Harmondsworth, Middlesex, England

First published 2000
1 3 5 7 9 10 8 6 4 2

Sheltie is a trademark owned by Working Partners Ltd
Copyright © Working Partners Ltd, 2000
All rights reserved

Created by Working Partners Ltd, London, W6 0QT

The moral right of the author has been asserted

Set in 14/22 Palatino

Made and printed in England by Clays Ltd, St Ives plc

British Library Cataloguing in Publication Data
A CIP catalogue record for this book is available from the British Library

ISBN 0–141–30802–8

Chapter One

'Yippee! Summerland Bay!' yelled
Emma excitedly. She threw her arms up
in the air and nearly knocked the cereal
box off the kitchen table.

Joshua, Emma's little brother, copied
his sister and waved his arms around
too.

'Summerbay, Summerbay,' he said,
giggling.

'Now, don't get overexcited,' said

1

Mum, smiling. 'Dad and I were only talking about *maybe* booking a week's holiday at Cliff-top Cottage. The same as we did last year.'

'Brilliant,' said Emma. 'And can we go and visit Mary at her animal hospital again?'

She jumped up from the table before getting an answer and headed for the door.

'I can't wait to tell Sheltie,' she said. Then Emma raced outside into the garden.

Sheltie, Emma's little Shetland pony, was waiting patiently by the paddock fence. He was rubbing his itchy chin against one of the sturdy wooden posts.

Emma swung her legs over the fence and sat on the top rail, with Sheltie's head resting in her lap. Sheltie's eyes twinkled as she scratched his chin and told him about Summerland Bay.

'We can ride along the sands and across the downs above the beach,' said Emma. 'And do you remember Mary?'

The little pony blew a soft whicker and pushed his muzzle into Emma's hand.

'Mary is that lovely lady who looks after all the animals,' said Emma. 'She's the one who removed that stone from your shoe when you went lame.'

Suddenly, Sheltie raised his front hoof off the ground and pawed at the earth.

Emma laughed. 'I think you *do* remember after all, don't you, boy?'

The little pony threw back his head and blew a long, wet raspberry.

'I think I'll write a letter to Mary and tell her we might be coming,' said

Emma. 'It's a shame she doesn't have a telephone. In the letter I'll tell her that you send a big kiss, Sheltie.'

Emma slid off the fence and Sheltie followed her across to his field shelter. He watched carefully as she filled up his hayrack. Then he nudged Emma playfully in the back as she forked over the straw and spread out a fresh layer of bedding.

'We'll have to ask Mrs Linney if we can use her friend's trailer again,' said Emma. 'And I'll have to get all your things ready and start packing right away. I've got a feeling we *will* be going to Summerland Bay.'

Sheltie rasped his tongue across the salt lick hanging from his stable wall, and bobbed his head up and down.

'Does the salty taste remind you of the seaside, boy?' Emma asked.

The little pony shook out his long shaggy mane and flicked the forelock out of his eyes.

'I think you're looking forward to Summerland Bay as much as I am!' said Emma, grinning.

One week later, Emma and her family were getting ready for their holiday at Summerland Bay. But they wouldn't be heading for Cliff-top Cottage where they stayed last year.

'The holiday cottage has been sold and the new owners are using it themselves at weekends,' said Dad. 'So instead, we're going to stay at The Golden Anchor, an old smugglers' inn sitting right on the beach.' He'd been keeping the news from Emma as a surprise.

'But the best bit is that it has its own stable,' added Mum. 'Sheltie will have a holiday home right on the beach too, and he'll be able to look out across the entire stretch of Summerland Bay.'

Emma's face lit up with excitement as she thought of all the fun she and Sheltie would have.

Mrs Linney had delivered Sheltie's pony trailer the day before and Emma had been loading bags of pony mix and hay into it. In fact, she had been busy packing and preparing all the things that Sheltie might need for his holiday. His saddle shone like a polished conker and hung with his bridle on special hooks behind the trailer door.

Now all the suitcases were packed and everyone was ready for an early start. Sheltie gave an excited snort as Emma led him up the ramp, with a clatter of hoofs. She tethered him safely inside the trailer. Sheltie's eyes

twinkled through the small window at the front. The window was open just a little so that the Shetland pony could enjoy the fresh air while they were travelling.

'It won't be long,' said Emma. 'You'll soon have the feel of soft Summerland sand beneath your hoofs!'

Sheltie blew a raspberry and licked the glass of his window.

It was nine o'clock when they finally set off, with Sheltie's little pony trailer trundling along smoothly behind the car.

Emma and Joshua waved goodbye to Little Applewood from the back. Joshua was strapped into his special car seat and clutching his bucket and spade.

As they drove along, Emma kept looking behind to make sure that the trailer was still there. She could see the tip of Sheltie's hairy muzzle poking through the window. Emma knew that Sheltie would be enjoying every minute of the journey.

After one quick stop to have lunch and to let Sheltie out for some exercise, they arrived at Summerland Bay. Dad suddenly turned the car off the main road and drove down a track towards the beach. Emma leant forward in her seat.

'Are we really going to be right *on* the beach?' she asked.

'You'll be able to dive out of the bedroom window right into the sea,' joked Dad.

Mum smiled. 'Don't tell her things like that!'

'Don't worry, Mum,' said Emma, laughing. 'I'm not *that* stupid!'

Chapter Two

Suddenly, the sandy track opened out on to the beach, and a shingle drive to one side led the way to The Golden Anchor's car park. Emma could see the little stable in the yard at the side of the inn.

'Look!' she cried. 'Sheltie's got a room with a sea view.'

'And a little sandy paddock,' said Mum. 'There's a small area fenced off from the beach, so Sheltie can be inside or outside.'

The little pony shook out his long shaggy mane and gave a really loud snort as he clattered down the ramp of his trailer. Then he raised his head and took a deep snuffling sniff of the sea air. Sheltie's nose twitched and he pranced on the spot. He was very excited to be back at Summerland Bay.

Once they had settled into their family room at the inn, Emma took Sheltie out for a ride.

'Guess where we're going?' teased Emma.

The little Shetland pony chewed on his bit. Then he jangled his reins and gave a happy whicker. He seemed to know exactly where he was going.

'Yes!' said Emma. 'We're going to visit Mary!' She tickled Sheltie's sides with her heels and let him lead the way. She thought it would be fun to see if he remembered the way to Mary's cottage from the beach.

Sheltie hurried forward and was soon trotting along the shoreline. He liked the feel of the soft sand beneath his hoofs, and danced along, with the surf splashing his legs.

At the end of the beach, some wooden steps climbed steeply up to the cliff-top. Sheltie hesitated in front of them. Then he looked at the nearby footpath. It was narrow in parts and dangerous, especially for a pony and rider. Emma remembered how Sheltie had rescued Alice Parker and her pony

when they got stuck on the same path
last year.

Sheltie seemed to remember this too
and chose the third route. It was much
longer but led along the bridle path

which skirted the beach, then wound its way gently up to the downs.

He flicked his long tail from side to side and set off at a steady pace.

It was quiet and peaceful up on the downs. Emma could see for miles across the soft, purple heather, which stretched away, like a rolling carpet, into the distance.

'I wonder if Mary knows we're coming to visit,' said Emma. 'I hope she got my letter.'

Sheltie answered with a belch.

'And I hope you'll watch your manners once we get there!' she added.

They followed the curve of the rising hill leading to Mary's cottage, with the warm sun on their backs.

Suddenly, the grassy downs ahead

sloped away into a big dip, just like a giant basin. And that was where Mary's cottage stood.

They looked down on the roof of the old tumbledown cottage. It looked exactly the same as it did when Emma and Sheltie had first set eyes on it. A narrow muddy path led to the front door of the cottage. Weeds and dandelions grew up all over the place.

'There's more ivy than last year,' Emma said to Sheltie. 'And some of it has started growing across the windows.'

Emma felt excited as she gazed down at Mary's home. She couldn't stop herself from grinning.

Woof, woof! The silence was broken by the lively barking of a dog.

Sheltie's ears flattened against his head. This was the bark of a dog that he didn't know. Sheltie's tail flicked from side to side as he waited for the animal making the noise to appear.

Emma laughed when she saw the cross-bred collie – the dog was all legs and lolling tongue. It scrambled up the path towards them, then threw itself on to its back, and lay there kicking its four paws in the air.

Sheltie lowered his head and nuzzled the pink belly that wriggled in front of him.

The collie dog leapt up and showered the little pony with licks. Then it sat back on its haunches and gazed up at Sheltie adoringly.

Sheltie scraped at the earth – and Emma laughed as the dog did the same.

'You're a cheeky thing, aren't you?' said Emma.

The collie dog just looked at her and pricked up its perky ears, listening.

Suddenly a familiar voice yelled from behind the cottage. 'Emma? Sheltie? Is that you?'

Chapter Three

Mary wandered out of the barn and into the sunshine. The old woman was cradling a chicken in her arms, and looked exactly the same as she did when Emma last saw her. She was dressed in a funny old raincoat, tied at the waist with string, and her smile was big and friendly.

Sheltie blew a loud snort of greeting, and the collie dog turned a somersault and hurtled back down the path, towards the cottage. The dog jumped up at Mary and got a peck on its head from the chicken she was carrying.

'Come on down, you two,' called Mary cheerfully. 'Come and say hello to Brindle properly.'

Brindle, the collie dog, sat at Mary's feet and waited for Sheltie and Emma to pick their way down the sloping path, into the little front garden. Mary put the chicken down in a wheelbarrow and came over to greet them both.

Sheltie shook his mane and whinnied softly as Mary scratched his ears.

'This is Brindle,' she announced. 'She's the latest member of my family.'

The collie dog raised a paw in

greeting as Emma slipped down from the saddle.

'Hello, Brindle,' said Emma as she shook the furry paw.

Mary lived in the tumbledown cottage by herself and cared for all kinds of sick and injured animals in her little hospital. Some people brought animals to the cottage for Mary to look after. And sometimes the animals came all by themselves – like Brindle.

'She just wandered in one day, dragging her hind leg,' said Mary. 'I think she must have been in some kind of road accident.'

Brindle looked up at her new mistress, with her pink tongue hanging out of her mouth.

'Anyway,' added Mary, 'that was two

months ago and she's been my constant
companion ever since. I've put up
posters, but no one's come to claim her.'

Sheltie was sniffing the collie dog's

head and licking Brindle's perky
ears.

'I think Sheltie likes Brindle,' said
Emma.

'Everyone likes Brindle,' said Mary,
smiling. 'She's such a lovely dog.'

'Do you still have Harold the goat
and Doris the donkey?' asked Emma.

'Oh, yes,' answered Mary. 'Harold
and Doris are still in their little field
behind the cottage. Come round and
see. We'll show you our new patients in
the hospital too, won't we, Brindle?'

Mary and her dog led Emma and
Sheltie down the side of the cottage and
around the barn to the animal hospital
at the back.

Mary's hospital wasn't a proper
hospital, but consisted of a few rows of

makeshift pens, cages and hutches, where injured or sick animals were treated and rested. They stayed there until they were fit enough to be released back to their own homes in the wild. All except Harold the hairy goat, with his poorly leg, and Doris, the old seaside donkey that nobody wanted any more. Both animals were like family to Mary.

As Emma looked round, she couldn't help noticing how run-down the place looked. Windowpanes at the back of the cottage were cracked. All the paint had peeled off the door. Some of the cages were tied together with string. And the pens and hutches which looked new last year were now tatty and in need of repair.

Emma also noticed that the roof of the old shed where Mary stored the animal feed was missing, and that the walls looked as though they would collapse at any minute. Struts of wood, pushed against the walls, seemed to be all that were holding the shed up.

Mary saw Emma's face. 'I'm afraid it's all a bit of a mess, isn't it?' she said. 'The animals cost so much with feed and vet bills, that I simply don't have any money left for the much-needed repairs!'

Emma smiled kindly. 'I wish I could help. I bet I could make some new hutches.'

'It's not that easy,' said Mary, laughing. 'I used to do all the work myself, but I'm getting old now. As you can see, I'm repairing the feed-shed. But I'm slow, and it's taking me ages.'

Just then, Sheltie wandered over to scratch his neck on one of the supports.

'No!' yelled Mary. 'Don't touch those, Sheltie, or the whole lot will come down. The roof used to hold the shed together. Now it's standing up with fresh air and a prayer.'

'Oh dear,' said Emma. She pulled on Sheltie's rein and led him away to meet all of Mary's new patients.

There was an orphan lamb, which Mary was raising for a farmer; two fox cubs, whose mother had been run over by a car; and five little rabbits. There was a goose with a swollen foot; a hen pheasant and her brood of fluffy chicks; and a funny squirrel with no tail, which Emma thought looked like a chipmunk.

'We had another goat last week,' said Mary. 'One of the wild ones living on the rocky cliff-tops. It just wandered in off the downs as bold as brass. There was nothing wrong with it – it just wanted feeding up, but I really didn't

have enough food left to give it.'

Emma decided then and there that somehow she was going to help Mary with her hospital and all the sick animals. She was going to think up a way of raising money to help towards the much-needed repairs. Otherwise Mary might not have a hospital any more. And then what would happen to all the sick animals?

Chapter Four

The next day, Emma and Sheltie spent
the morning on the beach with Mum,
Dad and Joshua.

Dad was busy making an enormous
sandcastle with Joshua, while Mum was
relaxing under a beach umbrella,
reading a book.

Emma sat down next to her. 'I can't
stop thinking about Mary's hospital,'
she said. 'You can't think of any

moneymaking ideas, can you, Mum?'

Mum looked up from her book and smiled kindly. 'I'll try hard to think of something.'

Overhead, the seagulls' cries echoed in the powder-blue sky. It was a beautiful summer's day.

'I think I'll take Sheltie for a ride along the water's edge to the end of the bay,' said Emma. 'Maybe I'll be able to think of something myself.'

Sheltie gave a loud snort and tossed his head as he pawed at the soft sand.

'You'd like a nice paddle, wouldn't you, boy?' said Emma.

'Don't go too far, Emma,' called Dad.

'And don't kick up sand if you gallop past anyone,' added Mum.

Emma smiled back over her shoulder

as she led Sheltie down to the water. 'I won't,' she called.

Joshua looked up and waved his bucket and spade. 'Bye-bye,' he shouted after her. 'Bye-bye, Sheltie!'

Emma mounted Sheltie and trotted him along in the foaming surf. There

was no one around so she pressed with her legs and urged the little pony into a canter. Sheltie's hoofs splashed through the lapping waves as Emma raced him down the beach to the end of the bay.

Giant rocks sloped away from the cliffs into the sea, and here Summerland Bay came to an end.

Emma dismounted, and kicked off her boots and socks. She rolled up her jeans and ran into the sea to paddle in the foamy waves.

It was great playing in the surf with Sheltie. But Emma still didn't have any moneymaking ideas to help Mary.

It was only when she was leading Sheltie back along the water's edge, with her socks dangling from her back pocket and her boots slung over Sheltie's saddle, that she thought of an idea.

'Driftwood,' said Emma. It was all around them on the beach. Emma suddenly remembered how, last year, she had painted a piece of driftwood that looked like a fish, and given it to Mary as a present.

'I can paint driftwood,' said Emma, 'and sell it as souvenirs to all the holidaymakers on the beach.'

Sheltie swallowed a piece of seaweed he had been chewing and gave a loud burp.

'Does that mean you don't think it's a good idea?' joked Emma.

The little pony blew some sand out of his nostrils and picked up a piece of driftwood in his teeth.

The wood was long, thin and twisted.

'It looks like a snake,' said Emma.
She took the driftwood gently from
Sheltie's mouth and studied it carefully.

'I could paint a lovely, snaky pattern
on this,' she said. 'It's brilliant, Sheltie!
Can you find another one?'

Sheltie answered with a cheeky flick of his mane. Then he rooted about in a mass of slimy seaweed and pulled out another piece of driftwood.

Emma reached out to take it. But Sheltie pulled away. Emma grabbed the piece of wood and pulled. Sheltie clamped his jaws tighter and pulled back.

'Oh. So you want a tug of war?' asked Emma. She pulled harder and Sheltie deliberately let go. Emma plonked down on to the sand with a bump.

Sheltie whickered noisily.

'I always fall for that trick, don't I?' said Emma, giggling. 'Now stop messing about and find me some more driftwood shapes.'

Sheltie was very good at this, and soon Emma had six really special pieces.

'If I ask nicely, maybe Mum will help me,' whispered Emma. 'She's really good at painting. Come on, boy, let's head back and get started.'

Back in their room at The Golden
Anchor, Emma laid all the driftwood
Sheltie had found on the bed for Mum
to look at. She told Mum about her
idea.

Sheltie was outside in his beach
paddock, tearing fodder from the hay
net on his stable wall.

'These are lovely,' said Mum. 'But
you don't want to spend all your
holiday painting!'

Emma pulled a face and looked
disappointed.

'It's a very kind thought, Emma,'
continued Mum, 'but I really don't
think it's a good idea you bothering
people on the beach.'

'They won't mind if they know it's

for the animal hospital,' protested
Emma.

'No, Emma,' said Mum sternly. Her
eyebrows were raised and Emma knew
that Mum was serious. 'I'll help you
paint these ones if you like,' said Mum.
'And you can take them back as
presents for Sally and your other
friends in Little Applewood. That's a
much better idea.'

Emma gave in and smiled. She could
see that Mum was right. Besides, she
would probably have to paint hundreds
of driftwood fish to make enough
money to help Mary properly.

'I'll paint them when I get back
home,' said Emma, 'on rainy days
when I can't ride Sheltie. I want to
enjoy every minute of this holiday, and

make the most of it while we're
here.'

But what Emma really wanted to do
while she was at Summerland Bay was
to help Mary's hospital. And she was
determined to think up another plan.

Chapter Five

That afternoon, Mum and Dad took Joshua to visit a tourist attraction in the next bay. It was a life-size model of an old pirate ship called *The Flying Dolphin*.

Emma didn't fancy looking around a model of a pirate ship, so she decided to visit Mary instead.

She rode Sheltie up on to the downs where they could see for miles over the cliff-tops and across the sparkling sea.

When they reached the rise overlooking Mary's cottage, Brindle was waiting. The collie dog must have known they were coming. She barked loudly and Sheltie pricked up his ears and answered with a whinny.

Emma and Sheltie followed Brindle round to the back of the cottage, where they found Mary sawing wood.

'Hello, Emma. Hello, Sheltie,' she called, looking up from her work. 'I'm making a start on the feed-shed roof.'

'Can I help?' asked Emma. She really wanted to do *something* for Mary and the hospital.

The old woman just smiled. 'I think I can manage,' she said. 'But if you really want to help, you can take Brindle for a nice long walk for me. She's getting under my feet and I've got a lot more sawing to do.'

The collie dog gave a loud bark and jumped up at Mary, knocking the saw out of her hand.

'See what I mean, Emma?' said Mary. 'She wants to help, but she's being a bit of a nuisance.'

Sheltie lowered his head and nudged the saw along the ground with his nose.

'Look!' said Emma. 'Sheltie wants to help too! It seems that everyone wants to lend a hand with the repairs.'

Mary clipped on Brindle's lead and looped the other end through Sheltie's stirrup leather.

The young dog was happy to pad

along next to her new friends as they
led her off on a walk.

Emma thought that Brindle might
like a good run along the beach. 'I bet
Mary doesn't have much time to take

you down into the bay, does she, Brindle?'

Emma guessed that the sharp bark meant 'no'. 'Come on then. We'll have a nice race across the sands and maybe a splash in the sea!'

Sheltie flicked his tail from side to side. Emma's little pony fancied a frolic in the surf too, and couldn't wait to get back down to the beach.

The tide was out in the bay, and the wide stretch of golden sand seemed to go on for miles.

Emma dismounted to unclip Brindle's lead and then hopped back up into the saddle. Sheltie lifted his hoofs high and danced through the surf, with Brindle chasing his heels. They trotted all the way along to The Golden Anchor, then raced back with the seagulls' cries ringing in their ears.

Sheltie and the little dog were enjoying every minute of their afternoon romp. But all the while, Emma was trying to think up another idea to help Mary with the hospital.

'I wish something fantastic would happen to solve all Mary's problems in one go,' whispered Emma to Sheltie.

Sheltie grunted and chewed on his bit noisily while Brindle cocked her head to one side and flicked up her perky ears. Both pony and dog seemed to be thinking.

Suddenly, as they neared the craggy rocks that marked the end of Summerland Bay, Brindle shot off.

'Brindle!' cried Emma. 'Here, girl!'
But Brindle didn't come back.

Sheltie flicked his mane out of his
eyes, then he pranced on the spot and
pulled on the reins.

Emma knew that Sheltie was trying
to tell her something.

'Can you bring her back, boy?' asked
Emma. Sheltie tugged on his reins
again. Emma quickly tucked them
through his bridle and dismounted. 'Go
on, Sheltie. Go and find Brindle.'

Sheltie trotted the short distance to
the end rocks. Then he ducked behind a
row of tall standing stones. And there,
waiting for him, was Brindle.

The collie had been digging a great
big hole and his nose and front legs
were covered in sand.

'There you are!' cried Emma as she found the two of them behind the rocks. 'I think it's time we took Brindle home, don't you, Sheltie?' she said, clipping on Brindle's dog lead. 'Mary's probably finished the roof by now.'

But Sheltie didn't want to go just yet. The little pony stuck his head in the hole and blew a loud snort. Then he

pawed restlessly at the sand. There was something very interesting at the bottom of the hole.

Sheltie lowered his head further, but he couldn't quite reach it with his teeth.

'What have you found that's so interesting?' asked Emma.

Chapter Six

Sheltie gave a sneeze and blew a puff of sand from his nostrils as he looked up.

Emma peered into the hole and saw something snake-shaped and smelly, like seaweed, coiled at the bottom.

'It's only an old rope,' said Emma. 'It's probably been buried down there for years.'

Brindle gave a sharp bark, and

Sheltie joined in with a series of noisy snickers.

'OK, OK,' said Emma. 'I'll get it for you.'

She knelt on the sand and reached down for the rope. It felt damp and rough as it uncoiled in her hand. But when she pulled on it, Emma discovered that the other end was buried deep beneath the sand. Emma pulled really hard but the rope didn't budge at all.

'There might be miles and miles of it buried beneath this beach,' she said. 'Or maybe there is something heavy tied to the other end.'

Sheltie blew a raspberry. The little pony seemed to like that idea. He nibbled at the smelly rope, then grabbed it with his teeth and gave it a hard tug.

'Do you want to have a pull too?' asked Emma.

Sheltie bobbed his head up and down, as if he were saying, 'Yes.'

'First I'd better tie Brindle up safely,' said Emma.

She looped the collie dog's lead over a pointed rock. She then tied the end of the rope to Sheltie's girth strap.

'Come on then, boy,' said Emma. 'Let's see just how long this smelly old rope is!'

Sheltie snorted and swung his head round to look at the hole. Then he started to pull. Emma stood in front and encouraged Sheltie forward.

The little pony braced himself and

then began to walk solidly towards her.
Emma watched the rope as it slowly
snaked its way out of the hole.

There seemed to be quite a lot of it.
Then suddenly the rope went very taut
and Sheltie had to pull really hard.
Slowly, bit by bit, he dragged the heavy
object out of its sandy grave. Emma
studied it.

'Wow! It's an old ship's anchor!' she exclaimed.

Emma untied the end of the rope from Sheltie's girth and the little pony trotted back to examine his find. He sniffed at the old anchor lying in the hole, then tossed up his head and blew Emma a raspberry.

Emma looked closely at the anchor again and tried to lift it. It wasn't a big, full-sized ship's anchor. It was quite a small one, just over half a metre long. But the anchor was very heavy and Emma couldn't move it at all.

She reached down and ran her hand over the knobbly surface. Then, with her finger, she traced the moulding on the anchor's shaft. It looked like a strange type of fish. The kind of fish

you sometimes see on the bases of old
lamp posts.

'It might be really old and valuable,'
said Emma.

Sheltie blew a snort and tossed back
his head.

Just then, Brindle started barking and pulling on her lead.

'We're coming,' called Emma. But Brindle couldn't wait. She tugged and barked and pulled on her lead until it worked loose. Then she ran off down the beach.

'Oh, no!' cried Emma. 'Not again.' She coiled the old rope as quickly as she could and pushed it back into the hole, on top of the anchor. Then she jumped into the saddle and urged Sheltie on.

Emma saw Brindle heading for the foot of the cliffs. Seconds later, the collie dog was on the footpath which wound its way up to the cliff-top.

Emma slowed Sheltie down to a trot. She had to think quickly. Should she follow Brindle up the cliff path? Or should she take Sheltie the long way round, up to the downs?

Emma was really worried. She couldn't bear to go back and tell Mary she had lost her new collie dog.

The cliff path was wide at the bottom where it left the beach. But as it climbed higher and higher it grew narrower and narrower. Emma and Sheltie had been on the top path before. They knew how dangerous and scary it was.

'We'd better go the long way up,' said Emma. 'Let's just hope that Brindle's gone straight home.'

She shortened the reins and sent Sheltie cantering along the bridle path leading up to the downs.

Eventually they were sailing down the shallow basin where Mary's cottage was hidden.

Brindle, the collie dog, came lurching out from behind the barn. She barked and barked and seemed very excited about something.

Sheltie whinnied anxiously. Something was wrong. Brindle's frantic barking was upsetting the little pony. He stomped a hoof and laid his ears back against his head.

'What is it, boy? What's wrong?' asked Emma.

Sheltie pawed at the ground.

'Has something happened? Is it Mary?' She called out at the top of her voice, 'Mary! Mary! Are you there?' But there was no answer.

Brindle ran to Sheltie and looked up at her new friend. Her sad whine told Sheltie to follow her.

Emma let Sheltie lead the way to the animal hospital at the back of the cottage.

There they found Mary, lying beneath a pile of rubble. Emma could hardly believe her eyes. 'No!' she yelled.

The feed-shed must have collapsed on top of her when she was fixing the roof. The old woman lay trapped beneath the shed walls.

It looked like Mary had hit her head when she fell. Her temple was badly gashed and there was blood trickling down her face.

Emma gasped and held her hand to her mouth. Then she leapt from the saddle and rushed to help.

Chapter Seven

Emma tried to pull the wooden wall
panels away from Mary's body, but
they were too heavy for her.

She knew there was no telephone
inside, so she couldn't ring for an
ambulance.

Suddenly Sheltie snorted noisily, and
nudged Emma on the arm. He wanted
to help.

'OK, boy!' said Emma. 'I'll get some

rope and you can help to pull this lot
clear. But first I need something to
bandage Mary's wound.'

She found a clean tea towel in the
kitchen and wrapped it around Mary's
head.

The old woman moaned softly and Brindle dived in to cover her with licks.

Emma gently pulled the collie dog away, then she tied some rope around the nearest wooden panel and fixed the other end to Sheltie's saddle.

Sheltie was a strong little pony, and the panels weren't too heavy for him. He walked forward slowly, with strong, solid steps and soon pulled the fallen walls away.

Mary didn't stir. She was breathing, but her eyes were closed and she seemed to be sleeping.

'Mary!' called Emma. 'Mary, can you hear me?'

Brindle whined and pulled at Mary's clothes with her forepaw. Sheltie lowered his head and blew at Mary's hair. But still she didn't stir.

'We've got to fetch help quickly, Sheltie. Mary won't wake up!' cried Emma.

The nearest house was Cliff-top Cottage, but Emma remembered that the new people just came down at weekends. They wouldn't be there today. The only thing to do was to ride for help.

Emma glanced back at Mary. Brindle had curled herself up against her and was keeping the old woman warm with her thick fur. Mary still hadn't woken up.

'We won't be long, Brindle,' said Emma. 'Come on, Sheltie.' She jumped up into the saddle and gathered the reins. Her hands were shaking, but she knew what she had to do. She had to take Sheltie down the cliff path to the beach below, and get help at The Golden Anchor.

Emma knew just how dangerous the cliff path was, but it was much quicker than going back down to the beach the long way round. And she could see that Mary needed help urgently.

Emma slipped out of the saddle and stood on the shoulder of the cliff. Sheltie placed one hoof on the narrow ledge of the path. Then he blew a soft whicker and bravely began the journey down to the beach.

'Be careful, boy,' whispered Emma. 'Take it nice and easy. One step at a time!'

Emma looked straight ahead and tried not to peer downwards at the sea and sand far, far below. Her legs felt like jelly as she followed behind Sheltie, holding on to his tail.

Sheltie was brilliant. He didn't falter once, but walked solidly on. To their left the path fell away to a sheer drop, with only the crashing waves below.

Butterflies the size of sparrows fluttered in Emma's stomach and she felt a bit sick. She spoke to Sheltie the whole time and this kept her occupied and made her feel braver. 'Well done, boy. Good boy, Sheltie,' she praised the little pony.

They made good progress and the path gradually grew wider and wider.

Then suddenly, Emma's mouth

dropped open. 'Oh, no,' she gasped.

Sheltie's ears flattened against his head and Emma stared hard at the pathway ahead. She could scarcely believe her eyes.

A big hairy goat was blocking their way. Its horns looked sharp and it stood

defiantly, ready to defend its territory. Emma knew that the goats lived and moved freely on the paths and cliff-tops. *This* goat had obviously decided that Sheltie was a threat.

It lowered its head and scraped at the rocky ledge with its hind hoofs. The goat was ready to charge.

For the first time, Emma glanced down to the beach. It was such a long way down and the path still wasn't wide enough for them to turn around. Sheltie blew a very worried snort. Suddenly they were in desperate trouble.

Just as Emma thought there was no way out, a blur of black and white fur shot between Sheltie's legs from behind.

It was Brindle. She charged forwards and placed herself between Sheltie and the angry goat. With snapping jaws, and nips and yaps, the collie dog drove the goat backwards. Then, like a true sheepdog, she sent the goat clattering away along the path and forced it down on to another ledge.

Emma didn't waste a second. 'Thank you, Brindle,' she called. Then she urged Sheltie forward again and swiftly carried on down the cliff to fetch help.

Chapter Eight

'Look! Sheltie!' yelled Joshua as Emma galloped up to The Golden Anchor from the cliff end of the beach. Mum and Dad had just returned from their trip to the next bay.

Sheltie had barely skidded to a halt on the shingle drive when Emma leapt from the saddle.

'It's Mary,' Emma blurted out. 'Mary's had an accident and she needs help!'

Mum and Dad listened carefully to Emma's story. Then Dad ran into the inn to phone the emergency services.

'I know you wanted to get down from the cliff-top as quickly as possible,' said Mum sternly, 'but it was a very dangerous thing to do. I want you to promise me that you will *never* do it again!'

Emma promised and gave Mum a big hug. At that moment, Dad returned and set out for Mary's cottage, with Mr Phillips, the owner of The Golden Anchor. They took Mr Phillips' Range Rover and drove off quickly in a cloud of dust.

'I hope Mary's going to be all right,' worried Emma. 'The feed-shed fell right on top of her.'

Mum looked very concerned too. 'It sounds as though the whole hospital is falling apart,' she said.

'It is!' exclaimed Emma. 'And it's awful! What will happen to poor Mary and all the sick animals if there's no hospital? I wish I'd been able to think of a way to help!'

'But you *have* helped,' said Mum. 'You and Sheltie were the ones who raised the alarm. And thanks to you two, the emergency services will be there in no time at all.'

'Mary's going to be OK,' said Dad as soon as he got back. 'She's had a nasty bump on the head,' he added, 'and the doctor says she's got to spend the night in hospital. But she's going to be fine.'

'What about the animals?' asked Emma anxiously. 'They'll starve if there's no one there to feed them!'

'No, they won't,' said Dad, smiling. 'Mr Phillips and I have already fed them. And tomorrow morning, we'll all go up there to check on everything before Mary comes home.'

'But what about Brindle?' asked Emma. 'What's happened to her?'

'Mr Phillips here is taking care of Brindle,' said Dad. 'She's downstairs in the stable with Sheltie, so you can stop worrying.'

But Emma *couldn't* stop worrying. Even when Mary came out of hospital there would still be all the repairs to take care of, thought Emma. And it was obvious now that Mary couldn't do the work herself.

In fact, Emma had been *so* worried about everything, she'd forgotten to tell Mum and Dad about the anchor that Sheltie and Brindle had found on the beach. So she told them now.

Mr Phillips seemed very interested indeed. 'I've always wanted a small anchor to hang up inside the Captain's Bar,' he said. 'An old ship's anchor would look really nice painted gold. If it's any good, I'll give you twenty pounds for it,' he offered.

'Wow!' Emma gasped. 'Twenty pounds for an old anchor.' Suddenly she had an idea.

'I'm going to start a collection for Mary's hospital,' she announced. 'Will that be all right, Mum?'

Mum nodded. She thought it was a wonderful idea. 'I'll make you a collection tin if you like,' she said.

'And I'll keep it on the bar counter,' said Mr Phillips.

'That's perfect!' said Emma. 'It means

the tin will be there collecting money for Mary's hospital all the time – even when we're back home in Little Applewood.'

Emma was so excited about the anchor that she could hardly wait to show Mr Phillips where it was.

She hurried downstairs to tell Sheltie and to get him ready. The little pony seemed to know that something exciting was happening. He pumped his little legs in the soft sand and blew a noisy whicker as she led him on to the beach.

Dad came along too, while Mum stayed behind to look after Joshua and Brindle.

'Lead on,' called Dad. 'Take us to the treasure.'

Emma grinned over her shoulder. 'It *is* treasure, isn't it?' she yelled back.

'It's worth twenty pounds,' said Mr Phillips, smiling. 'So it's a treasure worth finding.'

'Come on, boy.' Emma urged Sheltie forward. But when they reached the rocks on the beach where Sheltie and Brindle had found the anchor, Emma was in for a big disappointment.

'Oh, no, Sheltie. Look.' The tide had swept right in and that part of the beach was now completely under water.

'We'll have to come back tomorrow,' said Dad. 'We'll come and find the anchor first thing, before we go and feed Mary's animals.'

*

Later that evening, before Emma went to bed, she drew a picture of the ship's battered anchor. She tried really hard to remember what the funny fish looked like on the anchor's shaft. When she had finished it, Emma showed Mum and Dad.

They both looked at Emma's drawing. Then they looked at each other.

'Does this remind you of something?' Mum asked Dad.

Dad nodded his head and raised both eyebrows. 'It looks exactly like it to me,' he answered.

'Exactly like what?' puzzled Emma.

Dad told Emma all about their day visit to the old pirate ship. With all the excitement they hadn't mentioned it up until now.

'*The Flying Dolphin*,' said Dad. 'That's what the pirate ship was called.'

'And there was a figurehead at the

front of the ship, like a strange fish,' added Mum. 'A sort of dolphin, I suppose.'

'But the interesting part was the anchor,' Dad continued. 'The ship was a reconstruction. It was made from parts of the original pirate ship that was wrecked on Summerland Bay hundreds of years ago –'

'But there was no anchor,' Mum butted in. 'They never found an anchor. So all they had was a picture of what it looked like.'

'And what did it look like?' asked Emma.

'Exactly like your picture,' said Mum and Dad together.

Emma's mouth dropped open. 'Do you think the anchor we found could

be the one belonging to the pirate ship?'
she asked excitedly.

'If it is,' said Dad, 'then it's worth a
lot more than twenty pounds.'

Emma looked puzzled.

'Apparently, the missing anchor is
made of gold,' said Mum. 'The inn here
is named after it – "The Golden
Anchor".'

Suddenly, Emma couldn't wait for
the tide to go out. She wanted to race
Sheltie along the beach to find out if the
anchor really *was* made of gold.

Chapter Nine

The next morning, they were all up bright and early. The wet stretch of sand shimmered like a mirror beneath the first rays of sunlight.

'Come on, everyone,' yelled Emma.

Sheltie blew a loud raspberry as Emma rode him along the beach.

They led Mum, Dad, Mr Phillips and Brindle to the rocks where they had first dug up the anchor. Joshua was riding high on Dad's shoulders and waving at all the seagulls.

'It was somewhere around here,' said Emma. She pointed to a spot where she thought the hole had been, but there was nothing there now. The rough tide had filled the hole with sand.

Sheltie blew a quiet snort.

Mr Phillips had a spade. He started digging.

'No, not there,' said Emma. 'More to the left.' The tide had changed things and the rocks looked different too. Great swells of sand were banked up against them and smaller rocks that weren't there before poked out of the beach.

Sheltie stretched his neck and pulled on the reins. Then he lowered his head and sniffed at the sand.

'Do *you* remember where it was, Sheltie?' asked Emma.

The little pony shuffled his hoofs and walked over to a spot three or four metres away from Mr Phillips. Sheltie scraped at the sand and pawed with his hoof until he made a shallow dip.

Then he took a good sniff and started digging with both hoofs.

'It's here,' cried Emma. 'Sheltie says it's here.'

'Are you sure?' asked Mr Phillips.

Sheltie raised his head and answered with a loud, noisy snort.

'Positive,' said Emma.

Mr Phillips went to work again with his spade and soon dug a nice big hole.

'Yes!' cried Emma as the smelly coil of rope sprung up from the sand.

Mr Phillips and Dad pulled on the rope and hauled the anchor up out of the hole.

It was very heavy, and the two men were huffing and puffing as they lay the anchor on the sand.

'But it's not gold!' exclaimed Mum. She sounded disappointed. 'It's a dull grey.'

Emma edged Sheltie closer for a better look. It was true. It was just an ordinary old anchor.

The little pony jangled his bit, then did something very strange. He lifted a hoof and swiped at the anchor several times.

Sheltie's iron horseshoe scraped against the anchor and a grey flake fell off.

Beneath the dull grey that had flaked away was a shiny yellow metal.

'Look at that!' gasped Mr Phillips. 'It's gold all right. But it's been covered with lead.'

'Gold!' whispered Emma. 'A real gold anchor.'

'We've found the missing anchor

from *The Flying Dolphin*,' cried Mr Phillips. 'And it's all down to you and Sheltie.'

'And Brindle,' said Emma. 'It was Sheltie and Brindle who found it.'

'Well, there's bound to be some kind of a reward,' said Mr Phillips. 'It's a valuable hidden treasure, after all.'

'If there is, then I'd like to give it to Mary for the animal hospital,' said Emma.

She was so excited at finally being able to do something to *really* help Mary and save the hospital. She gave Sheltie a big hug and buried her face in his thick mane.

'We've done it, Sheltie. We've really been able to help,' she said.

Sheltie blew a thundering snort. He

seemed to know exactly what Emma was saying.

'Talking of Mary,' said Mum, 'we'd better put this anchor somewhere safe and then go and feed her animals.'

Sheltie helped drag the anchor along the beach, and back to the inn. Mr Phillips then locked it safely away in Sheltie's stable.

Within minutes, Emma was back in the saddle, urging everyone to hurry up. 'Come on, let's go,' she called. 'We've got all the animals to feed now!'

Mum and Dad smiled at each other as they climbed into Mr Phillips' Range Rover.

'We'll lead the way,' yelled Emma. Then she flicked the reins and Sheltie galloped ahead.

*

Mary came home that afternoon. A few days later, on the day Emma and Sheltie left Summerland Bay, Emma presented her with a nice big cheque from the Historical Society, outside The Golden Anchor Inn.

'I don't know how I can ever thank you,' said Mary. She gave Emma a big hug and ruffled Sheltie's mane as Dad led him up the ramp, into the pony trailer.

Brindle didn't seem to want Sheltie to go, and jumped into the trailer with him.

Sheltie nuzzled the collie dog's head as Emma knelt down to give her a hug.

'Bye, Brindle. Be a good girl and look after Mary,' whispered Emma. Then she led Brindle out and got into the car.

'Goodbye, Emma. Goodbye, Sheltie. Come back soon,' called Mary as she waved them off. Brindle barked noisily.

'We will,' Emma called back. And from inside the trailer came the longest, loudest raspberry that she had ever heard!

READ MORE IN PUFFIN

For children of all ages, Puffin represents quality and variety – the very best in publishing today around the world.

For complete information about books available from Puffin – and Penguin – and how to order them, contact us at the appropriate address below. Please note that for copyright reasons the selection of books varies from country to country.

On the World Wide Web: www.penguin.co.uk

In the United Kingdom: Please write to *Dept. EP, Penguin Books Ltd, Bath Road, Harmondsworth, West Drayton, Middlesex UB7 0DA*

In the United States: Please write to *Penguin Putnam inc., P.O. Box 12289, Dept B, Newark, New Jersey 07101-5289* or call 1-800-788-6262

In Canada: Please write to *Penguin Books Canada Ltd, 10 Alcorn Avenue, Suite 300, Toronto, Ontario M4V 3B2*

In Australia: Please write to *Penguin Books Australia Ltd, P.O. Box 257, Ringwood, Victoria 3134*

In New Zealand: Please write to *Penguin Books (NZ) Ltd, Private Bag 102902, North Shore Mail Centre, Auckland 10*

In India: Please write to *Penguin Books India Pvt Ltd, 11 Panscheel Shopping Centre, Panscheel Park, New Delhi 110 017*

In the Netherlands: Please write to *Penguin Books Netherlands bv, Postbus 3507, NL-1001 AH Amsterdam*

In Germany: Please write to *Penguin Books Deutschland GmbH, Metzlerstrasse 26, 60594 Frankfurt am Main*

In Spain: Please write to *Penguin Books S. A., Bravo Murillo 19, 1° B, 28015 Madrid*

In Italy: Please write to *Penguin Italia s.r.l., Via Felice Casati 20, I-20124 Milano*

In France: Please write to *Penguin France S. A., 17 rue Lejeune, F-31000 Toulouse*